Fight

by

Chris Powling

Illustrated by Alan Marks

Published in 2006 in Great Britain by
Barrington Stoke Ltd
www.barringtonstoke.co.uk

Copyright © 2006 Chris Powling
Illustrations © Alan Marks

ISBN-10: 1-84299-414-X
ISBN-13: 978-1-84299-414-6

Printed in Great Britain by Bell & Bain Ltd

A Note from the Author

There are more ways than one to be a bully. That's what this story is about – how a little guy can sometimes bully a big guy. It's based on a fight that really did happen.

I know because I was there ...

For Patience Thomson,
with thanks for all her help
with this story

Contents

Chapter 1
True Story

All boxers know this saying:

The bigger they are, the harder they fall.

It's a load of rubbish.

Here's what they should be telling you:

The smaller they are, the better they fly.

That's much more like real life. Take my word for it. And take my word for the story you've got in front of you. It happened just the way I describe.

Well, most of it did.

Maybe I've changed a few bits here and there. You'd do the same if you felt the way

I do. Even now my face goes red with shame when I remember the worst fight I ever had.

Chapter 2
Best Mates

I've never been much of a fighter. I'm too small and skinny for one thing. All it takes to blow me off my feet is a sudden gust of wind.

There's something else as well. The truth is I'm not very brave. I may act all

cool and cocky. But that's only for show. If there's a chance I might get hurt ... well, you won't see me for dust.

This pleases my mum no end. "Thank goodness you're not a tough guy, Matt," she said one morning. "You never come home with a black eye or a split lip. I hope that doesn't change when you go on to Upper School. It's a place that's full of tough guys."

"I'll keep away from them, Mum."

"Promise me?"

"Well, I'll do my best."

"Leave the rough stuff to the other kids. That's my advice. And go around with someone who's bigger than you. That way you've always got some back-up."

"Like Eggy, you mean?"

"Eggy?"

Mum looked at me and smiled. She'd always had a soft spot for Eggy. "Is Eggy going on to Upper School?" she asked. "I thought you were the only one."

"Just the two of us, Mum."

"Matt, that's great! You won't be on your own, after all. You'll have Eggy looking after you."

"And he'll have me," I said.

Mum gave me a funny look. She's not the sort of mum who thinks her own kid is perfect. "Yes, he'll have you," she nodded. "Let's hope you don't let him down."

"Why would I let him down?"

"Matt, most of the time you're a great kid. But you love getting your own way. And you throw a wobbly when that doesn't happen. It's why you're so fond of Eggy. He always does everything you tell him."

I didn't listen any more.

Mum was bang out of order. Eggy had been my best mate for ages. He'd *always* done what I told him. Why would he want to change things now we were starting at Upper School?

Chapter 3
Eggy

Eggy had been born big, you see. Really big. Every bit of him loomed with bigness – his body, his legs, his head. Yes, even his head. Eggy had a head like Humpty Dumpty.

Now don't get me wrong here. Eggy's head was big, all right. But Eggy wasn't cocky at all. "You know my problem, Matt?" he'd say with a groan. Kids only have to look at me and they think I'm a tough guy."

"Well, fancy that!"

"Matt, it's not a joke. How would you like to be my size? I try really hard to be normal. And it just doesn't work. Somehow, whatever I do, I end up being *scary*."

Scary?

Eggy was a lot more than scary. When you saw him lumbering towards you it was hard not to turn and run. Trust me, that's what most kids did. "Hey!" Eggy shouted after them. "Where are you going? I only want to talk!"

By then they were out of sight.

And I can't say I blame them. Not when they saw how huge he was. Eggy once lifted a see-saw onto his back in a single heave.

I'm talking about a proper see-saw here. In
a proper children's playground. It had two
little kids on it at the time – one at each
end. I'm not surprised they were wetting
themselves.

So why didn't Eggy scare me?

The reason for this was simple. I'd
sussed him long ago. Deep down, Eggy was
just plain *nice*. He hated being such a
giant. "Suppose I forgot what a hulk I am,
Matt?" he often asked me. "What do you
think would happen then?"

17

"You'd pick up another see-saw," I smiled. "Only this time the kids at either end would fly off into orbit!"

"You reckon?" said Eggy.

He looked close to tears when he said this. It made me feel really bad. I'd been teasing him all day. That's why he'd lifted the see-saw onto his back in the first place. Eggy had never said no to me. Not once. He'd do anything to stay my best mate.

Anything at all.

That's what I was betting on at Upper School.

Chapter 4
Upper School

Upper School isn't famous. It's not posh or sporty or bookish. I bet you know a school just like it. Most of it is grey and stony – stone walls, stone steps, stone floors. The teachers are grey and stony, too. I bet the head-teacher chose them so they blended in. "Grey," said Eggy, on our first day there. "Everything in this place is grey, Matt."

"And stony," I said.

"Yeah," said Eggy. "Stony as well."

We were dressed in our new school uniforms. These made us look grey and stony, too. Not that Eggy blended in. The other first-years looked ready to run for their lives. "What kind of kid are you?" one of them said. "Some sort of freak?"

"Just tall for my age," said Eggy.

"And still growing," I grinned. "Right, Eggy?"

"Eggy?"

"That's his nick-name. It comes from the shape of his head. Looks just like an egg!"

"So I see!"

"Can we call you Eggy, too?" another kid asked.

"If you want to," Eggy said.

We had first-years all round us by this time. Eggy was making his mark as he always did. This was just what I wanted, of course. Suddenly, a red-haired boy with glasses grabbed Eggy's arm. "Hey," he said. "Haven't I heard about you?"

"About me?" said Eggy.

"Didn't you pick up that see-saw in the park? With some kids still sitting on it?"

"Only a teeny see-saw," said Eggy.

"Oh, really? I suppose the kids were teeny as well."

"Yes, they were."

The boy with the red hair grinned. By now you could have heard a pin drop. Every kid in the school yard was gaping at Eggy. They couldn't take their eyes off him.

You could see the see-saw in the park getting bigger and bigger in their minds. You could see the teeny kids turning into teenagers to match.

Then the bell rang for our first class.

You can bet I stayed close to Eggy. He looked crushed by all the fuss. As for me, I was smiling from ear to ear. This back-up of mine was magic. He'd keep me safe from the tough guys all right. So far, my plan was spot-on.

Chapter 5
Tough Guys

We saw five fights in our first week at Upper School. Most were just huffing and puffing. But they still pulled in a crowd. "Tough guys," said the red-haired kid with glasses. "Or kids who want you to think they're tough guys."

"Why?" Eggy asked.

"Why what?"

"Why do they want to be tough guys?"

The red-haired kid looked at Eggy. "You tell me," he said. "You're a tough guy yourself, aren't you?"

"Am I?" said Eggy.

"Tough as old boots," I said. "Eggy could give any kid at Upper School a kicking they'd never forget."

"Could you?" asked the red-haired kid.

"If I wanted to ..." Eggy said.

"So do you want to?"

"No," said Eggy. "I don't."

"Why not?"

"He's saving himself," I said, quickly. "For a fight that really matters. Not the feeble stuff we've seen so far. It's not worth clenching his fists for punch-ups like that."

"He's waiting for a real tough guy, eh?"

"Yes, he is."

"That's not true – " Eggy began.

I gave him a dig in the ribs. This red-haired kid was getting to me. Why was he asking Eggy all this stuff? Had he spotted that my best mate wasn't nearly as scary as he looked? If so, I'd better get it sorted fast. "Listen, Eggy," I hissed. "Let's find a bit of space, OK? We need to talk!"

"Have I done something wrong, Matt?"

"Wrong?"

I let the word hang in the air. I could see from Eggy's face that he knew how cross I was.

Chapter 6
The Dustbins

I found the space we needed near the grey and stony kitchen block. No one would bother us there. Not with the dustbins so close. You could smell them all round us – a stale, fatty stink of old grub. I glared at Eggy. "Do you want to spoil everything?" I asked.

"Me?" Eggy blinked.

"Yes, *you.*"

My best mate looked puzzled. He shifted from one foot to the other and scratched his chin. You could almost see his brain ticking over. This was just like Eggy. He'd always been slow to take things in. "*Think* about it," I snapped.

"Think about what, Matt?"

"About the tough guys," I said, gritting my teeth. "This place is full of them, remember? Our only hope is to be harder than they are. You and me together."

"Together?" said Eggy.

"Together, that's right. I do the thinking. You do the tough stuff. That's how it works, OK?"

"Not any more."

"Sorry?"

"You can count me out, Matt. I'm fed up with scaring the other kids. It makes me feel like some kind of bully. And I'm not. I never have been. I just happen to be big, that's all."

I stared at him in horror.

Had I lost my back-up already? Without Eggy, I could see what was coming at Upper School – black eyes and split lips for a start. I felt a shiver run down my spine. But I was careful not to show my panic. I put on my

most cool and cocky voice. "Anything else
you want to change?" I asked.

"My name," Eggy said.

"What?"

"Eggy," said Eggy. "The nick-name you
gave me, Matt. I've always hated it. I want
my proper name back."

"Your proper name?"

"That's right."

"But you haven't had a proper name for yonks. I can't even remember what your proper name is."

"Neither can I," Eggy grinned.

It was the grin that did it, I suppose. It made the whole thing seem like a joke. So I just couldn't help myself. I hit him smack on the nose. Yes, me. Small, skinny me – the gust-of-wind kid.

The kid who loved to get his own way.

Chapter 7
Fight

It was like a chimp duffing up a gorilla.

Eggy shrugged off every punch I aimed at him. His eyes were wide with alarm. "Matt, don't do this!" he begged. "I'm twice your size. You won't get anywhere fighting me."

"Who says?" I sneered. "Take a swing, OK? Hard as you like. That's if you've got the guts."

"Matt, this is stupid!"

"Just hit me, right?"

"I can't, Matt."

"You can't? Gone all soft and runny, have you? That's just what I'd expect from a kid called *Eggy.*"

"Stop calling me that, OK?"

"Eggy!" I yelled. "Eggy! Eggy! Eggy!"

"Matt, I'm warning you ..."

His warning was just for show. I knew he wouldn't really hurt me. He wasn't that kind of gorilla. But I was that kind of chimp. I'd got myself in a right old state. My arms were spinning like windmills. My fists went rat-a-tat on his chest. Eggy didn't even bother to dodge, let alone hit me back.

When did the other kids arrive?

Maybe they'd been there all along. At first I thought they were cheering me on – you know, little guy against big guy. This made me fight even harder. I tucked in my chin. I skipped this way and that. I let fly with jabs and hooks and upper-cuts. No wonder the noise around us got louder and louder.

Then I saw they were all laughing.

They were laughing at me, not Eggy.

"Look at the temper on him!" someone shouted.

"Talk about a tantrum!"

"He'll be bashing himself up before long!"

"Or have a heart attack!"

"Think we should call 999 just in case?"

Eggy was shaking his Humpty Dumpty head. This wasn't what he'd wanted at all. Suddenly, he grabbed me round the waist. I couldn't move in such a gorilla-like grip. "Matt, stop it," he said in my ear. "Let's call the fight a draw. That OK with you?"

"A draw?"

"So there isn't any loser, Matt."

"Who says there isn't a loser?" I spat. "You're the loser, Eggy. Because you'll always be *Eggy*, Eggy!"

I saw at once I'd made a mistake.

Eggy stood very still for a moment.
Then he took a deep breath. I felt him shift
his grip. This made me punch and kick
even more. It didn't do me a blind bit of
good. I was still locked in his arms as he
carried me towards the dustbins. Luckily,
the one he'd chosen was empty. But it still
smelled like a pig-sty when he lifted the lid.

It smelled even worse when he dropped
me inside.

I stayed there till break-time was over. By then, I stank like old grub myself. The School Nurse had to send me home for a change of clothes.

"For a change of attitude, too," she said.

Chapter 8
Alfy

See what I mean about a little guy taking on a big guy? Kids who are my size don't have a hope. Anyone who tells you different is living in a dream world.

Mind you, it really is different at Upper School now.

No one dares start a fight, for one thing. You might end up in a dustbin. Alfy will see to that. And since Alfy is as big as a brick lavvy, everyone's keen to do what he says. Even our grey and stony teachers seem a bit scared of him.

But I'm not.

These days, Alfy's my best mate again. I don't think of him as Eggy any more. And he never uses the nick-name that I seem to have got at Upper School.

"Proper names only, Matt," he always says. I only wish the other kids agreed with him. They use my nick-name all the time. With them, it's the nick-name or nothing.

'Tough Guy' is what they call me.

For some reason they think this is funny.

Barrington Stoke would like to thank all its readers for commenting on the manuscript before publication and in particular:

Tom Davies-Evans

Mrs Ruth Garbett

Charlotte Hayman

Diana Osborn

Rupert Potter

Rhys Sykes

Become a Consultant!

Would you like to give us feedback on our titles before they are published? Contact us at the address below – we'd love to hear from you!

Email: info@barringtonstoke.co.uk
Website: www.barringtonstoke.co.uk

Also by the same author ...

Blade
by Chris Powling

STAY AWAY FROM TOXON.
That's what they tell Rich.
They tell him about the Blade
too, and what it can do to you.
But Rich is in the wrong place at
the wrong time.

You can order *Blade* directly from our website at
www.barringtonstoke.co.uk

If you loved this book, why don't you read ...

Speed
by Alison Prince

THE NEED FOR SPEED

Deb loves to drive fast.

The faster, the better.

Until she goes too far, too fast ...

gr8reads